LITTLE MISS SPLENDID
and the house with a view

Original concept by Roger Hargreaves
Illustrated and written by Adam Hargreaves

MR. MEN   LITTLE MISS

MR.MEN™ LITTLE MISS™ © THOIP (a Sanrio company)

Little Miss Splendid and the house with a view © 1998 THOIP (a Sanrio company)
Printed and published under licence from Price Stern Sloan, Inc., Los Angeles.
This edition published in 2014 by Dean, an imprint of Egmont UK Limited,
The Yellow Building, 1 Nicholas Road, London W11 4AN

ISBN 978 0 6035 6780 3
54226/2
Printed in Great Britain

All rights reserved. No part of this publication may be reproduced, stored in a retrieval system, or transmitted,
in any form or by any means, electronic, mechanical, photocopying, recording or otherwise,
without the prior permission of the publisher and copyright owner.

Little Miss Splendid looked out of her very splendid window, set in her most splendid house, at her very splendid garden, and smiled.

And then she frowned.

Little Miss Splendid looked out of her window every morning and every morning she smiled and then she frowned.

And what made her frown?

I'll tell you.

At the bottom of her garden, on the other side of a small stream lived Mr Mean.

Unlike Miss Splendid's very large and most splendid house Mr Mean's house is very small and very run down.

A not at all splendid house.

In fact, the most un-splendid house one could ever imagine.

Mr Mean was the sort of person who did not like spending money, especially on his house.

Little Miss Splendid was the complete opposite.

And she did not like having Mr Mean as a neighbour.

His house quite ruined her splendid view.

It was on this particular morning as she stood looking out of her window that Miss Splendid had an idea.

She rang her builder, Mr Trowel.

"Hello," she said. "This is Miss Splendid. I would like you to build a wall for me. Come at once."

Mr Trowel came over within an hour and within a day he had built a wall at the bottom of Little Miss Splendid's garden.

A high wall.

A wall that hid Mr Mean's house.

Now, Mr Mean also liked to look out of his window each morning.

He had a splendid view of Miss Splendid's extraordinarily splendid house.

And what made the view all the more splendid for Mr Mean was the fact that it hadn't cost him a penny.

Mr Mean was very unhappy when he looked out of his window the next day and all he could see was a high, red brick wall.

But as he stood there looking out of his window Mr Mean had an idea.

The next morning when Little Miss Splendid looked out of the window she couldn't believe her eyes.

There was a huge hole in her beautiful wall and through the hole she could see Mr Mean's ramshackle house.

Miss Splendid was furious.

She rang Mr Trowel immediately and by lunch-time Mr Trowel had rebuilt the wall.

But the next morning there was another hole in her wall.

And so it went on all week.

Overnight Mr Mean would knock a hole in the wall and the next day Mr Trowel would come and repair it.

And then one morning the whole wall had disappeared.

But not just the wall.

There was no sign of Mr Mean's house either!

"That's strange," said Miss Splendid to herself. She put on her best hat and went to investigate.

When she got down to where Mr Mean's house had been she heard the sound of building coming from the other side of the hill. She climbed to the top of the hill.

And for the second time she couldn't believe her eyes.

There was Mr Busy putting the finishing touches to a house that looked liked hers, but was even more splendid!

"Looks good, doesn't it?" said a voice behind her.

It was Mr Mean.

"What ... what ... how?" spluttered Miss Splendid.

"It was all those bricks that gave me the idea," said Mr Mean and grinned. "All those free bricks!"

Little Miss Splendid didn't know what to say.

So she didn't say anything.

And she went home.

To her splendid house.

A splendid house, but no longer the most splendid house!